Lisa Bastien & Lori Bastien

MINOR KEY SIGNATURES

THEORY BOOSTERS SERIES

ISBN-10: 0-8497-7380-6
ISBN-13: 978-0-8497-7380-8

ORDER OF SHARPS

Trace the order of sharps in both clefs.

NAMING KEY SIGNATURES
MAJOR SHARP KEYS

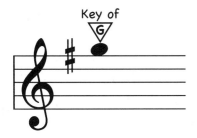

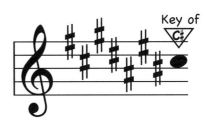

1. Name the last sharp: **F♯**
2. Name the next letter **up** in the music alphabet: **G**
3. The answer is: **Key of G Major.**

1. Name the last sharp: **B♯**
2. Name the next letter **up** in the music alphabet: **C** C is already sharp.
3. The answer is: **Key of C♯ Major.**

Name each Major key signature.

1. __DM__

2. _____

3. _____

4. _____

5. _____

6. _____

RELATIVE KEYS

For each key signature there are two keys, one is Major (M) and one is minor (m). The two keys for each key signature are called **relative keys.**

NAMING KEY SIGNATURES
MINOR SHARP KEYS

1. Name the Major key: **D**
2. From the Major key, D, count down three half steps:

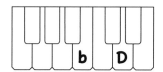

3. The answer is **b minor.**
4. D Major and b minor are relative keys.

1. Name the Major key: **F#**
2. From the Major key, F#, count down three half steps:

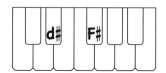

3. The answer is **d# minor.**
4. F# Major and d# minor are relative keys.

Hint: The letter names of the relative Major and minor keys are always one alphabet skip apart:
ⓒM • ⓐm or ⓖM • ⓔm

MATCHING

KEY SIGNATURE FUN

Name each Major and minor key.

1.

____0____ sharps.

[C] M   [a] m

2.

_____ sharp.

[ ] M   [ ] m

3.

_____ sharps.

[ ] M   [ ] m

4.

_____ sharps.

[ ] M   [ ] m

5.

_____ sharps.

[ ] M   [ ] m

6.

_____ sharps.

[ ] M   [ ] m

7.

_____ sharps.

[ ] M   [ ] m

8.

_____ sharps.

[ ] M   [ ] m

A. Name the relative minor key for each Major key below.
B. Match each surfboard to its key signature.

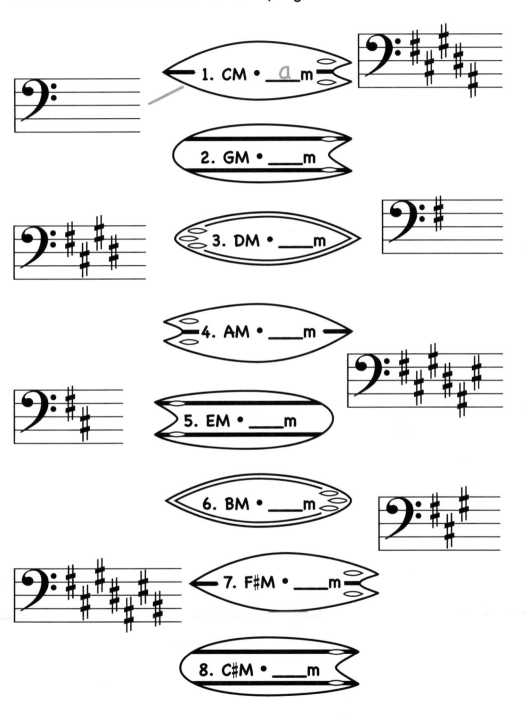

1. CM • __a__ m

2. GM • ___ m

3. DM • ___ m

4. AM • ___ m

5. EM • ___ m

6. BM • ___ m

7. F#M • ___ m

8. C#M • ___ m

Name each Major key signature and write it on the staff.

1. 1 sharp
   Key of ___G___ .

2. 7 sharps
   Key of _____ .

3. No sharps
   Key of _____ .

4. 4 sharps
   Key of _____ .

5. 6 sharps
   Key of _____ .

6. 5 sharps
   Key of _____ .

7. 3 sharps
   Key of _____ .

8. 2 sharps
   Key of _____ .

Put the following relative Major and minor keys in order from keys with the fewest number of sharps to keys with the most number of sharps.

DM • bm

CM • am

EM • c#m

F#M • d#m

GM • em

AM • f#m

BM • g#m

C#M • a#m

1. _CM • am_

2. _____

3. _____

4. _____

5. _____

6. _____

7. _____

8. _____

ORDER OF FLATS

B E A D G C F

Trace the order of flats in both clefs.

FUN FACT!

The order of flats is the order of sharps spelled backwards.

F • C • G • D • A • E • B

B • E • A • D • G • C • F

A. Write the order of sharps on the staff.

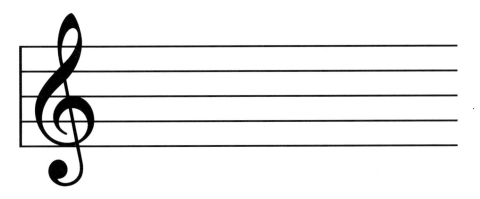

B. Write the order of flats on the staff.

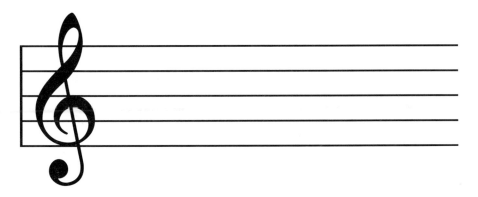

NAMING KEY SIGNATURES
MAJOR FLAT KEYS

1. Name the next to last flat: **E♭**
2. The answer is: **Key of E♭ Major**

1. Name the next to last flat: **D♭**
2. The answer is: **Key of D♭ Major**

EXCEPTIONS

Key of C is accidental free!

Key of F has just **B♭**, no more than that!

NAMING KEY SIGNATURES
MINOR FLAT KEYS

1. Name the Major key: **D♭**
2. From the Major key, D♭ , count down three half steps:

1. Name the Major key: **F**
2. From the Major key, F, count down three half steps:

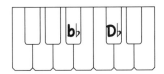

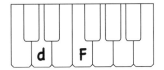

3. The answer is **b♭ minor.**
4. D♭ Major and b♭ minor are relative keys.

3. The answer is **d minor.**
4. F Major and d minor are relative keys.

MATCHING

1.

2.

3.

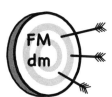

4.

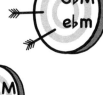

5.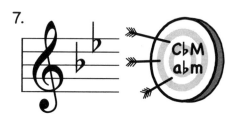

6.

7.

8.

KEY SIGNATURE FUN

Name each Major and minor key.

1.

 _1_ flat.

F M   d m

2.

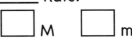 ____ flats.

☐ M   ☐ m

3.

 ____ flats.

☐ M   ☐ m

4.

 ____ flats.

☐ M   ☐ m

5.

 ____ flats.

☐ M   ☐ m

6.

____ flats.

☐ M   ☐ m

7.

____ flats.

☐ M   ☐ m

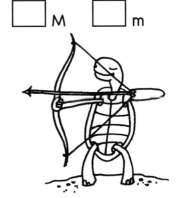

KP25

KEY SIGNATURE SOCCER

Name the relative minor key for each Major key.

1.

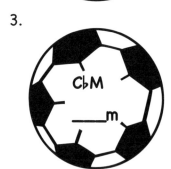

FM

___d m

2.

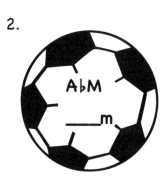

AbM

___ m

3.

CbM

___ m

4.

DbM

___ m

5.

BbM

___ m

6.

CM

___ m

7.

GbM

___ m

8.

EbM

___ m

Match each soccer ball from the previous page to its correct goal.

1. _8_

2. _____

3. _____

4. _____

5. _____

6. _____

7. _____

8. _____

Q: What kind of meal does a Valentine like?

A: A "hearty" one!

FOR YOUR INFORMATION...

THE CIRCLE OF FIFTHS

The **Circle of Fifths** shows the relationship between relative Major and minor keys, and the number of accidentals in their key signatures. The **Circle of Fifths** is based on the fact that beginning with any pitch and moving up by intervals of fifths (C, G, D...) will eventually lead back to the starting pitch.

Start with C Major/a minor and follow the circle **clockwise,** moving **up by fifths.** Notice that one **sharp** is added to the key signature each time you get to a new key.

Start with C Major/a minor and follow the circle **counter-clockwise** moving **down by fifths.** Notice that one **flat** is added to the key signature each time you get to a new key.

Three keys overlap in the circle: B/Cb, F#/Gb, and C#/Db. These keys are called **enharmonic keys** because their pitches sound the same on the piano but are named and written differently.

WRITING MINOR KEY SIGNATURES

Example: Key Signature for e minor

1. From e minor, count **up** three half steps to find the relative Major key:

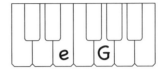

2. Write the key signature for the relative Major key:

Write each minor key signature and fill in the name of its relative Major key.

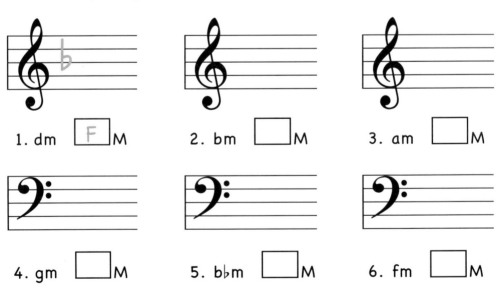

1. dm ☐F☐ M   2. bm ☐☐ M   3. am ☐☐ M

4. gm ☐☐ M   5. b♭m ☐☐ M   6. fm ☐☐ M

7. cm ☐M   8. em ☐M   9. b♭m ☐M

10. f♯m ☐M   11. c♯m ☐M   12. g♯m ☐M

Q: Why wasn't the teddy bear hungry?

A: Because he was stuffed!

Fill in the missing part of each exercise.

1. CM 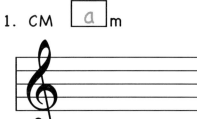 m

2. G♭M 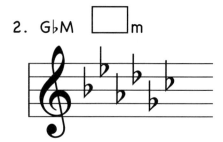 m

3.  M•fm

4. DM•bm

5. FM•dm

6. C♭M 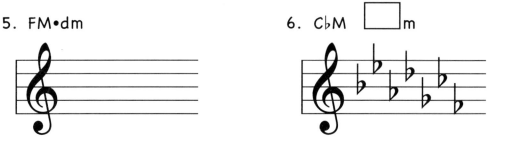 m

7. B♭M ☐m

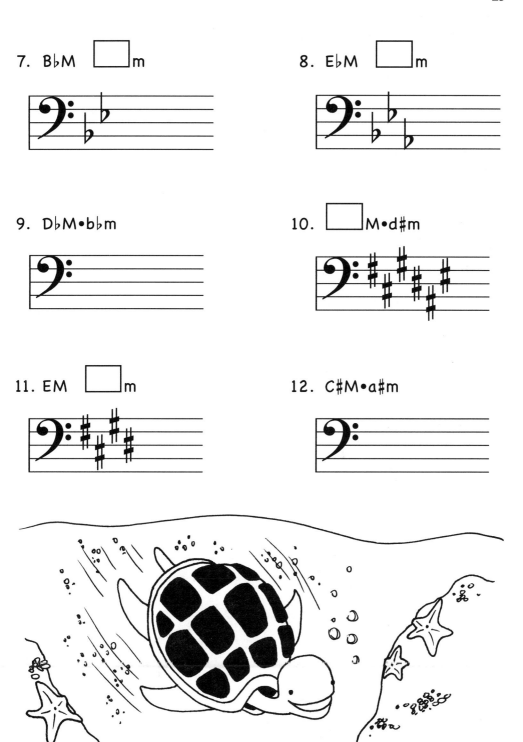

8. E♭M ☐m

9. D♭M•b♭m

10. ☐M•d♯m

11. EM ☐m

12. C♯M•a♯m

RELATIVE KEYS

Match each minor key to its corresponding relative Major key.

WHO AM I?

1. With three sharps in my key, **who can I be?**

   ☐ M ☐ m

2. Two flats are me, and my minor key is g, **who can I be?**

   ☐ M

3. I've got four sharps and a Major key of E, **who can I be?**

   ☐ m

4. If my minor key is b, **how many sharps would you see?**

   ☐ sharps.

5. Four flats is a lot, that's what I've got, **who am I?**

   ☐ M ☐ m

6. My Major key is F, and I've a minor key of d, **how many flats describe me?**

   ☐ flat(s).

26

Name each relative minor key.

1. CM [a]m

2. A♭M [ ]m

3. FM [ ]m

4. BM [ ]m

5. G♭M [ ]m

6. E♭M [ ]m

7. AM [ ]m

8. EM [ ]m

9. DM [ ]m

10. GM [ ]m

Q: What do you call a really smart pair of pants?

A: A "jean"ius!

Here's another way to find the relative Major key from a given minor key.

Example: Find the relative Major key for **a minor.**

1. Write the **a minor** triad:  ←— 3rd
2. The third of the minor triad names the relative Major key.
3. Answer: **C Major.**

Shade in the third of each minor triad and write its name in the blanks below.

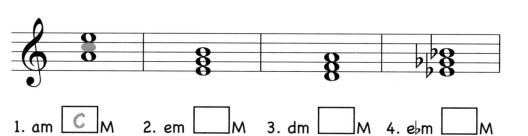

1. am [C]M   2. em [   ]M   3. dm [   ]M   4. e♭m [   ]M

5. bm [   ]M   6. fm [   ]M   7. cm [   ]M   8. f♯m [   ]M

KEY SIGNATURE MEMORY

Write the letter name of the correct glove from the
following page to match each key signature below.

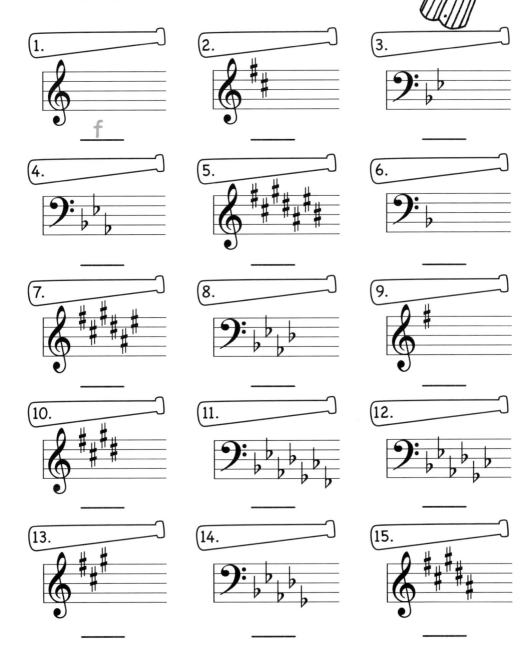

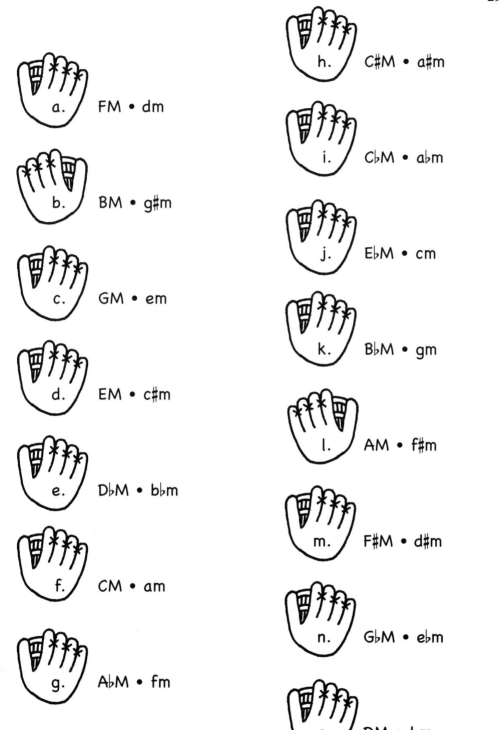

a. FM • dm

b. BM • g#m

c. GM • em

d. EM • c#m

e. DbM • bbm

f. CM • am

g. AbM • fm

h. C#M • a#m

i. CbM • abm

j. EbM • cm

k. BbM • gm

l. AM • f#m

m. F#M • d#m

n. GbM • ebm

o. DM • bm

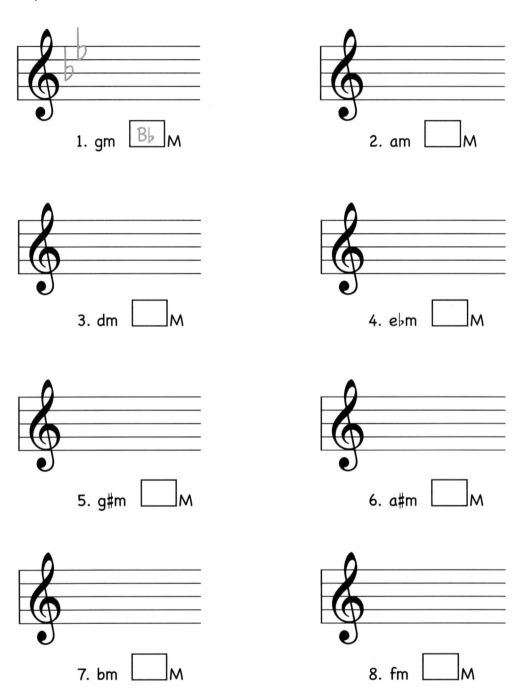

30

Write each minor key signature and name each relative Major key in its blank.

1. gm [B♭]M

2. am [   ]M

3. dm [   ]M

4. e♭m [   ]M

5. g♯m [   ]M

6. a♯m [   ]M

7. bm [   ]M

8. fm [   ]M

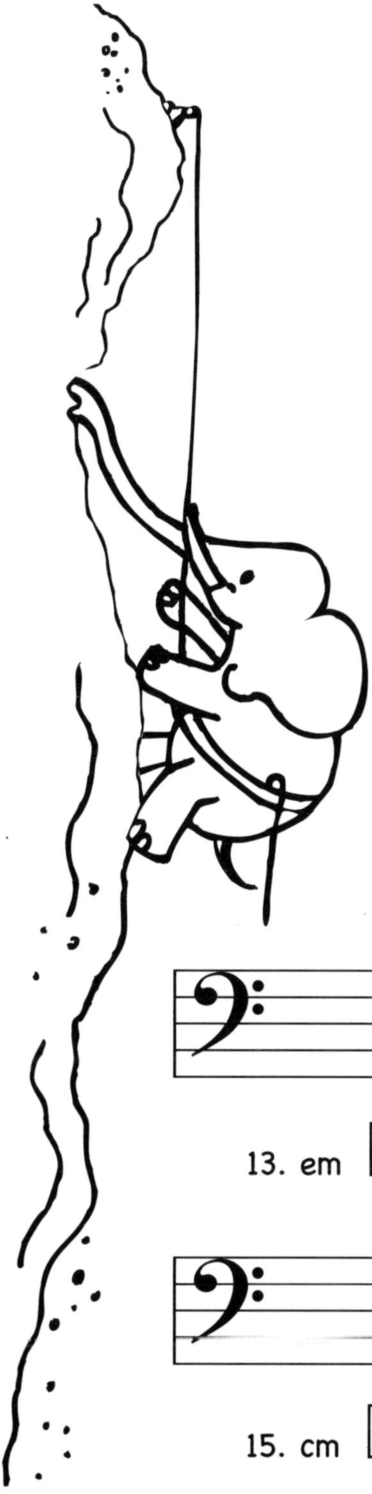

9. f#m ☐ M

10. b♭m ☐ M

11. c#m ☐ M

12. d#m ☐ M

13. em ☐ M

14. a♭m ☐ M

15. cm ☐ M

Two! Four! Six! Eight!

Minor keys are really great!

Name and write them, you can do,

We are really proud of you!

_____ has learned to recognize

and write minor key signatures!

_____

Teacher's Signature